AMERICA-CRY FREEDOM

CULTURE SHOCK ESSAYS II

By
I.C. Moore

Bookman LLC
Publishing & Marketing

Providing Quality, Professional Author Services

www.bookmanmarketing.com

Contributions:

ACKNOWLEDGEMENTS:

To my wife Bridgette and daughter Brittany who are my constant inspirations.

DEDICATION:

Ships are the great Religions
Poets the lifeboats.
Every sane man I know has
Had to jump overboard...

Hafiz

TABLE OF CONTENT

THE COLOR OF JAZZ

Without filters-
Pour the amber of your soul
Inside the tones of
Vibrating colors.
On a
stave of reason
Walk your bass scent through
The chamber of eyes-
No posturing for sound is necessary.
You suffer
through chord progressions in
Half-truths of poetic imagination.
The color of jazz punctuates
The brass blues of a morning glow.
Fragile-
A piano bends notes along walls
Teasing the ivory tremors
From under a cape of green.
The opal bass throbs.
The pink vocals scream.
The yellow rhythm section explodes!
When the
fumes
of harmony settle
Color, rhythm and humanity
Converge at song's end
Blessing the unity of many flavors
Resonating through the echoing
Symphony of crystal light.

<u>INTRODUCTION</u>

Come back!
We never left the silence of tomorrows.
Come back!
The yesteryears bounce forward
Always striding, bullying the future.

It was on a gray drizzly London morning that the *CultureShock* took its first bite of my consciousness. Spiteful and depressed I squeezed out the rain and came face to face with my lost past.

It was here, in the crumbling ruins of Strawberry Hill. A name that conjures up a time of indulgent privilege and noblesse oblige, where the good citizens interviewed prospective homeowners into their select band of bigots.

Here, among the overgrown moss, layering the once petite nearby railway station, that I heard my first *CultureShock*, a return journey, year later, to my school of yesteryear. Looking down the track I realized that no longer would guilt-ridden parents be riding this route to see their little abandoned children detained by the pleasure of Lord Shaftsbury's benevolence. This endowment of charity, spewed from the loins of culpable ninetieth century politicians.

The haunt from which my emotions of early manhood had rebelled, Fled, cursed, despised and battled hard to forget.

This curse of impregnated cultural denial that formed a steel net of fear and self-doubt around my bursting aspirations. It all looked so small now. It's difficult to conceive how these same bricks, mortar and pathways could have held me in such awe, such trepidation! I felt now

I could crush the whole place in my hand, like some discarded pulp mail.

> The elegant Georgian mansion stood aloof. The center clock still kept its immaculate time. The broad sweep of the giant fir tree still dominated a beautifully manicured lawn mowed with military precision.

But the school buildings had gone. The sounds and smells of trenchant orders and burnt oatmeal were squashed between new housing tracts, displacing the old soccer field. On this field I had led soccer teams, blending blood and sweat together through ice and snow, heat and rains. Bringing back on many occasions respect for this school of lost souls. All the hopes of my youth had been turned under the sod, like the desecration of Cartage. Nothing remained of the spirit but the salt in the wounds. Yet the maturity of my consciousness was still hidden in shadows and the limbo of aloneness.

> I hungered to be born again on that gray morning of purpose. That insipid drizzle outside was my Baptism to a new faith!

A faith, in myself as a worthy human being-wrapped in the skin of many cultures. A faith, that reconciled color with history and the pursuit of happiness. A faith, that taught the discipline of the reed, silently observing the waters of life, unfolding its ebbing rhythms of human understanding.

> The *CultureShock* spirit was a Vibrating rhythm of resonating Sensation, that preached the Message of *Sankofa*-the faith that one can only go forward if one has understood the past'!

COMING TO AMERICA

Ships coming from a distance carry everyone's dreams ashore. For some they slip in with the eddies of the tides. For others they crash against the rocks of poor fortune. Each brings their new song of freedom, coming to America.

When I first visited New York and stumbled over the stacks of garbage on the corners of Fifth Avenue, I was in awe of such poverty side-by-side with such wealth. I later discovered that the city was going broke; and that New Yorkers were betting on the city's demise. Years later when I flew into San Francisco I was greeted by quite the opposite spectacle. My wife's sister picked us up in her 350 SL Mercedes and ferried us through a kaleidoscope of dazzling billboards advertising everything from gambling in sun-baked Reno, to giving humanitarian aid to El Salvador. I was deposited, after a ride across the elegant Bay Bridge, at Lake Merritt, the pride of Oakland's Afro-American bourgeoisie; I had to pinch myself to believe the opulence was real.

It was real. The Afro-American community of Oakland, California, is probably one of the richest black communities in the world. The skyline houses that look down from the redwood hills of the East Bay are not the exclusive preserves of whites, as is often the case in many neo-colonial lands. The sun-drenched Mediterranean climate is host to one of the most diverse communities in America. Yet beyond the mortar and bricks of their homes, Afro-Americans own very little of the wealth of this fertile region.

On my arrival in Oakland, California I learned how the city was scorned by San Francisco, the city across the bay, as all cities inhabited by people of color in the white world are scorned. Oakland's population used to be over 60% Afro-American, but it has now shrunk to below 45%. Yet the racist tag has stuck and Oakland continues to be subjected to innuendoes of second-class citizenship. This abuse only serves to highlight the cruel irony of history; that Oakland was the celebrated start of the Trans-Continental railway which was built to bring Easterners to the gold of the Sierra Nevada. But the fame of the whoring town of 'Frisco had spread too wide for the truth to be known-that San Francisco was just a stop-over place for far more rewarding adventures. It was not, however, until I began to work with Americans that I got to see the people behind their veils. Stripped of a reason to care, people often don't. Settled people become addicted to their immediate gratification's and interest in and about others becomes disturbingly absent. The public persona of Americans being the embodiment of the perfect lifestyle is a veneer, which fools nobody least of all someone new to the country eager to dig beneath the surface with every question. American lifestyles are so tied to credit and debit and the obsession with crime, that to come to America is to feast on dreams of fabled opportunities and harsh demoralizing realities.

My first encounter with Americana came after I pounded the streets for a month, looking for a comparable position as an Engineer, which I'd held in London; I was told by an agency interviewer in no uncertain terms, that "as a black man I could not hope to get a position that would allow for vertical mobility. I could only hope for lateral movement!"

American racism strikes foreigners with such bold frankness that on first impressions its comes as a relief from the hypocrisy of the British class system.

Yet the acceptance of conflicts between racial groups in America is so prevalent and reveals an attitude of such bitterness, that it floods every fiber of the nation's structure. All sides tug, push and pull for a louder voice to express their mutual detachment. Short of Civil War, nowhere in the world is bitterness for one's fellow citizens such a basic part of the psyche of the nation, as it is in America. Most startlingly, it is a bitterness that believes it's the most victimized in the world. Trying to explain the 1000 year-old war between the Scottish and the English, to an Afro-American, is to be reduced to redundancy. Afro-America prides itself on being history's biggest victims, as if no other group black or white could possibly have suffered so much!

I was finally saved from the grip of this consuming form of racism by the guiding hand of patronage; in the land of the brave and the free it's not what you know but who you know! A cousin of my wife just happened to be on the local school board. He found me a job as a janitor at a junior college where I eventually worked for four years. In the course of my apprenticeship I was exposed to American supervisors who took more than 2 years to summon the verve to have a conversation with me beyond, "What's 'appen'". It took me sometime to realize that as a black Englishman I frustrated the majority of Americans who I met, because I didn't fit into a neat box, i.e., White, Black, Asian, Hispanic or Other. It reminded me of when I first filled out a visa form to come to the USA; I had to grapple with questions that asked me what my grandparent's ancestry and religion were? Whether any of my distant relatives had committed a crime for which they weren't convicted? And what was my race? I resisted this attempt to be made into a racist, as long as I could, but I was encourage and impelled by American's bureaucracy to view myself in this one-dimensional form.

Try as I might, however, my accent set me apart and my attitude really seemed to upset my supervisors so much so that they were always finding ways to mess with me. In social interactions too, my accent (or American accents reacting to my English drew attention. As a result I was subjected to a wide range of responses ranging from people staring at me-mouth opened in disbelief, followed by them storming out of the room muttering "who is that nigger?" too; women approaching me and asking me to "just say som'thang". The former I lost no sleep over. The latter I learned to live with.

After these teething times of acculturation, a process that everyone goes through in learning another culture, I was swept up by the vibrancy of Afro-American life in Oakland. The bubbly familiarity of Afro-American life is an intoxicant to the newcomer. Particularly when that newcomer has come from a European tradition that considers any display of emotions to be 'uncivilized'.

For a Black man who had lived in isolation and cultural persecution in England, America represented a land flowing with milk and honey. Just the fact of seeing prosperous black people strolling the streets was enough to get the heart pumping with pride and self-worth. The daily acknowledgment of Afro-Americans for each other in the streets, introduced me to a brotherhood' I'd not known before. The encouraging expressions of warmth in the language instilled an emotional bond that resurrected my wounded soul. It seems to me that the Afro-American world of the East Bay was just a kiss away from paradise.

Yet as a Black individual who has traveled and lived in other Black countries, my assimilation into Afro-America has been the most difficult. Firstly, because it seems to me that Afro-America binds all people of color to its knee-jerk reaction for survival, without necessarily knowing what is the best way to survive? And secondly, Afro-America is inflexible to alternative solutions aimed at doing more than just surviving. For example, throughout the world the people of color understand they are the victims of a discrimination acted out on them. It is understood that those who do the discriminating (The Man, The whites, Them, Etc.) are robbed of the one thing they seek to take from us-their humanity. When we play their game of hate and bitterness, we deliver up to them that which they seek, and ensure our own slavery. Thus when Afro-Americans use derogatory words to describe each other, they are not inventing a unique cultural language, rather they are propagating the language of slavery. Nothing disgusts a foreign black more than to hear an Afro-American refer to himself and his kinsmen as a 'nigger'. This is no solution. Rather it is a papering over of the hurt of humiliation, a sublimated denial of the self as a deserving, feeling human being. It is also not a solution when intelligent Afro-Americans mimic Ghettoize to impress their friends as to just how 'Street Black' they are. It seems to me that respect and love for oneself has to be the number one priority for any people. For a people who have been enslaved both physically and mentally, respect and love must be approached as a religious commitment.

I found it difficult settling into America because I made the mistake of thinking America would be just like Britain, "people speak English, don't they?" However, beyond the surface similarities the nations are very different. For example, the educational system in Britain, perhaps because of its elitist program of directing students into academic or vocational courses from an early age, instills a deep reverence for knowledge in its students. In my own case, I was a complete failure in school and spent the latter part of my teens erasing the humiliating experience from my memory. Nevertheless, as I matured and went in search of my own character and purpose, I dipped back into the basics that had been etched on my soul, the basic belief that truth and knowledge would make me free but required my active involvement to guarantee it. In America education seems to be just another option among many, not necessarily central to an individual's advancement. The Government's reluctance to establish a national test of intelligence for its schools, conflicts with the 'free market' values promoted by business leaders, which have lead to a history of duplicity and enslavement for the majority. The result, consequently, is the promotion of the few over the many. With those who can grab the most being the arbiters of rightness and taste.

For a foreigner America's unique, diverse, culture defies traditional society norms. While most countries are united by the sameness of their people, ideas, religions, character, and behavior, America defines itself and is defined by others, by its obsession with being different from each other. But the differences are only on the surface, for Americans are of one mind when it comes to all others, here and abroad, and that is they always consider themselves Number 1.

The Anglo-Saxons may still control the corridors of power in America, but the pulse of the nation is in its streets of explosive ethnic diversity. It's like a nation that's reaching for the sky, just to surrender.

Coming to America the voyager is suspended between the dream of freedom and the reality of slavery, a freedom that offers credit to include everyone in the scheme of things, and a slavery that compels conformity to debt. America is a freedom whose passion is out of control. Yet its very confusion is the catalyst, which sparks great adventures. America is an emotion that claims objectivity, believing hopelessly in the theoretical rights of man. Yet as the real world of finite resources encroaches on America's glut of power, it will only be America's resilience to change that promises it a special place in the world of the future.

THE ARRIVAL

And I came
Naked
Free
Burned by destiny's anthem
Yet cloistered by the fire of my desire spitting apples out
towards the horizons
That shrunk away from my tremendous commitment to
Suck up all my disappointments
And mistakes and
Imbibe them with the pregnancy of a new Birthing!

Come then
Into this fire of cleansing power!
Burn away the warts of
Transgressions and fears!
Embrace the silent hour
Of our arrival-
Here brother,
Sip
cool waters.

OBSERVATIONS OF AMERICAN BEHAVIOR FROM FOREIGN VISITORS

These comments below reflect the thoughts of people from around the world and do not represent the governments or political positions of their countries. Rather they are the first impressions of individuals traveling to America and responding honestly and openly about how they are made to feel when encountering the American culture.

Visitor from India:
-Americans are in a perpetual hurry, don't allow themselves leisure time to enjoy life.

Visitor from Ethiopia:
-Americans are explicit; they want a YES or a NO.

Visitor from Kenya:
-Americans are distant, not close to other Americans.-Individualism is high.
-Unless you ask a question, they won't look at you.-American students are restless, inattentive, rebellious, and the teachers have poor class discipline.-Parents are too preoccupied with work, can't spend time with their kids.
-There is widespread neglect and abuse to kids.

Visitor from Iran:
-Americans use the word "friend" loosely, it doesn't imply close ties or real bonds.

Visitor from Vietnam:
-Americans are really handy, even the women.-Americans are friendlier to strangers, but don't always care about family members.

Visitor from the Philippines:

-Children are very forward in their speaking.   They have no respect for elders.

-Children don't offer help to their parents willingly, they either have to be told, or be rewarded with some kind of compensation.

Visitor from Korea:

-Teachers give students too many choices, even for the kind of assignment to do. And the students still don't do well.

THE CULTURE OF HISTORY

The Culture of History is an exploration of where we have come from and where we are going. It is a perspective of a neglected but vital aspect of our story on this planet, which daubs us with the mark of our birthplace.

> Are we the victims or the villains of our history?
> And how much do we perpetuate blindly the dictates of
> a past we did not create?

The Culture of History is often the unseen hand of our trail of suffering through this world, which reinforces our present and undermines our future.

> The Culture of History is the victors' story written on
> the backs of their victims, as a mark of progress and
> righteousness?

For this reason and others, History has been the dark tunnel of fear that ordinary human beings have lingered within, in the hope of seeing the light of their dreams through shadows. History's legacy has been the manipulation of forgetfulness and pain by the power brokers of materialism. History's victims have become the hurt creatures of regret, toiling in their ignorance of the past and their fear of the future.

> The Culture of History is made bold by the significance
> of cultural identity, recognizing that it is only with a
> strong self-sense of culture that we can be free!

For cultural history joins the past to the present and the future, offering tales of growth and struggle on a universal and personal level.

Cultural history informs us of the flavors of that struggle, and shows us that our most creative moments have come through struggle.

We are informed in our youth that we can never go forward unless we understand our past, and that to comprehend our origins gives power to our present. More specifically, we are told that *'those who refuse to learn from the past are condemned to repeat it'*.

Yet the adage is reflected in every daily Newspaper headline. Are we thus caught up in an adolescent mindset where to receive advice is to immediately reject it as divisive?

Has the "Youth Now" campaign of the commercial advertisers succeeded so well that everyone is devolving back to adolescence for fear of reaching maturity? Nothing, it seems, can reverse the self-inflicted disease of stupidity, masquerading as nationalism, as we regress into the 21st Century!

Some nations have so much history that their recorders have a vested interest in embellishing the tall tales of nationhood.

Other nations, victims of a devastating past, want to forget their history as soon as possible, as if amnesia will make the consequences of the past just disappear?

And yet others, still relatively young in nation building, wish only to be measured by today, unwilling to accept that there has been many today's in the past, which have resulted in their current predicament.

Yet it is equally important we demand that the history we learn about our collective past be accurately upheld, and seen in the context of the larger human story, not just the expediency of current jingoism's. Because history is the story of all of us.

> The Culture of History represents a supreme irony for a civilization like our own, that prides itself on the principals of science and engineering. Indeed it can be said that Newton and Descartes stride across our pragmatic world with pride. It is therefore curious that when it comes to History, we are prepared to suspend the logic of Newton's third law of physics: *"to every action there is an equal and opposite reaction!*

To wit, what has happen in the past has had a direct impact on the present! We are living in a world formed before we came here, that will survive our deaths and effect other peoples lives long after we are gone. Yet we treat history as some kind of fatalistic dome beneath which we strut in a dream consumed by our thirst for flitting ecstasies, while babbling about family values, God and national pride?

> Are we so consumed by our fears of impotence, that all we will leave behind will be the debris of our regurgitated phlegm?

So why the unconnected ness, the divided soul of mind and body pulling in opposite directions? The behavior of selfishness masquerading as leadership?

Perhaps past pain has crippled us? Perhaps we are trapped by the Machiavellian mindset of those we allow to lead us? Perhaps because of our ability as human beings to delude ourselves into thinking that what is physically before our eyes, is always more important that the knowledge of our experiences!

> Our ability to deceive ourselves when it comes to looking back into our own histories, let alone the nations', is part of the problem. But we also have an

15

inordinate ability to believe the worst about themselves, and particularly when it comes to evaluating own experiences. And by the worst, I mean our self-evaluation is rarely lucid or logical. We have come to be comforted by pain and fear, perhaps guilt is a better word.

Our pain marks our trail of 'existence' through this life. Religion without faith has a lot to do with this, but self hate adds its spice to the mix!

When we understand that we are all creating history daily, we are reminded of the words of the great poet Hafiz:

> *Now is the time for the world to know*
> *That every thought and action is sacred*
> *Now is the time to understand*
> *That all your ideas of right and wrong*
> *Were just a child's training wheels?*
> *To be laid aside*
> *When you can finally live*
> *With veracity*
> *And love.*

<u>DEMOCRACY IN AMERICA</u>

In democratic communities, each citizen
Is habitually engaged in the contemplation
Of a very puny object: himself.
If he ever raises his looks higher,
He perceives only the immense form
Of society at large or the still more
Imposing aspect of mankind.
His ideas are all either extremely
Minute and clear or extremely general and vague:

What lies between is a void.

When he has been drawn out of his
Own sphere, therefore, he always
Expects that some amazing object will
Be offered to his attention; and it is on
These terms alone the he consents to tear
Himself for a moment from the petty,
Complicated cares that form the charm
And the excitement of his life.

Alexis de Tocqueville

17

I.C. MOORE

THE CULTURE OF LANGUAGE

The Culture of language is the first talisman of cultural identity; a community's distinct symbol of identity that presents the first barrier to open communications with the larger human family. Yet it is also the essential vehicle for articulating our similarities. A language is the people! Robbed of language, humanity has no special significance over the other creatures of the earth.

> Yet language is a living entity, a combination of sounds and words that stretch back to the first utterances of mankind. In this sense the world's languages have many common roots.

However, these roots have been lost to the present-day practitioners who, rejecting their history, choose to measure their particular language by the political and military conquests of their leaders.

> We live now in an environment where the Culture of Language is increasingly being manipulated by groups within society who seek desperately to find their unique voice, in a world dominated by global commerce.

While corporate entities seek to bridge the divide between global commerce, cultures suffer. Indigenous languages are undermined daily in the name of commerce. Commerce, however, which has always been a positive conduit for cross-cultural fertilization, is now so desperate for money and markets, that its dynamic hegemony pushed all else asides as it seeks out pliant consumers?

> The language of TV, particularly MTV, has so engulfed the world that language that was developed on the ghetto streets of America-a language that is created to separate the victims from the oppressors-is now being used by middle class kids in Tokyo suburbs?

Within the host countries of the United States and Western Europe, the youth are being encouraged to develop idiosyncratic languages that have nothing to do with communicating ideas beyond a commercial hip ness. The phenomenon of Rap Music and the African American experience is a desperate attempt on one level to communicate something "real" to the larger society that is only interested in materialism. Yet 70% of Rap music is sold wholesale to white youths that can only relate to this phenomenon as a consumer fashion statement?

> The Culture of Language is fed back into the real
> African American community-the majority of black rap
> performers are middle class-which develops a hybrid on
> a hybrid and increased pressure on real black people to
> be re-synthesized into a charicature for popular culture?

The Culture of Language today is a testament to our lack of meaning, as nations, societies, groups and sub-groups concoct their own babble in an attempt, not to communicate-but to objectify themselves as a new cult, worthy of being bought out by some desperate, debt-ridden Conglomerate?

EBONIC PLAGUE
by James Cagney

Stick em up, fool
punk yo'self
gimme all the adjectives you got!
Yo—there's a shortage of words on the street
and I'll be damned if I let me babies go
speechless
for another week!
This is a literary asswhoopin, G
a social abortion of Biblical proportions!
What?!?
Good Evening, Daddy!?!???
Ain't you HEARD?!?
there's a PLAGUE ON in the streets, fool!
Spread by
inarticulate rats
and
illiterate fleas!
The language has been TAINTED!!!
Words
have been divided
between
us   and   them
the haves and the ain't gots
and we're running low
and running scared
and if this keeps up,
My family won't be able to
EXPRESS THEMSELVES!!!
So hurry up, punk!
you betta come up off some
INTRANSITIVE VERBS
IDIOMATIC PREPOSITIONAL PHRASES

or imma pop a CAP in yo ASS!!!

WE INTERRUPT THIS ROBBERY ALREADY IN PROGRESS TO
BRING YOU THE FOLLOWING PAID PROGRAM

AMAZING DISCOVERIES!
This program is rated TV-UA
and may not be suitable for Unrealistic Audiences

FADE IN:
This is the Ghetto. (Insert Yanni Music)

The Ghetto. Home to Drugs, Poverty, Teen Pregnancy.

and…BROKEN   ENGLISH!

Meet Kwame.

Kwame can't do math,
cause he buys his 40 dog and bags of weed
with exact change.

Kwame can't read,
cause the only books on his
shelf at home is a book of food stamps
and it's EMPTY

Kwame can't speak
cause the only words he ever heard
since he was born have been
SHUT UP, NIGGA & SIT YO' ASS DOWN!!!
His daddy works collecting aluminum cans in affluent
neighborhoods except on Sundays when he can bee
seen strolling downtown begging for 'Social Change'.

22

His momma, meanwhile, is a full-time, highly trained,
professional CRACK ADDICT and part-time PROSTITUTE
with a heart of gold who spends her weekend mornings
studying Cosmetology classes at Laney.

With parents like these, it's no wonder Kwame's English
skills have become lax! Kwame's teachers' agree:

"Kwame has the **POTENTIAL**
to become a **GOOD STUDENT**
but sometimes it's just hard to **REACH HIM**
because he so obviously speaks a **DIFFERENT LANGUAGE**
from the other (assimilating monkeys swinging from
dry-cleaned trees in downtown Hercules.)"

That is, UNTIL NOW!

Once upon a time,
Kwame used to SKIP SCHOOL
and SMOKE WEED
but now, thanx with the help of
HOOKED ON EBONICS
Kwame's communication skills
have increased TENFOLD!
Currently, Kwame attends
classes EVERYDAY and earns
sparkling D's and F's and now **YOU CAN TOO!!!**

YES!!! With these EAZY LISTENING TAPES
soon, you too will be able to *spit wicked game* such as:
I Be Finna Go To Tha' Sto
or
Is You Be Pregnant Fo Sho?!?
(and of course, the ever popular)
I Ain't Be Got No Weapon, Offisuh…

Yes! **HOOKED ON EBONICS!**
and if you call our **TOLL-FREE NUMBER 1-888-DUH-OU812**
in the next 20 minutes, we'll throw in
HOOKED ON CAJUN and an **AMOS' N ANDY** T-shirt
FO FREE!!!   FO' FREE!!!   FO FREE!!!

And now, here's
Jane Seymour—star of TV's
DR. *QUINN, MEDICINE WOMAN*
to tell you more!

MEANWHILE IN A COFFEEHOUSE ACROSS TOWN
This is NOT A POEM!!
This is a VERBAL MUGGING!!
This is a CALL TO ARMS!!!

We are a nation of MINOR people
Who are either invisible or on diss-play
At the Smithsonian between the dodo bird and the spotted owl.

The Government has Star 209'ed us back into Jim Crow
Cuntry!
The Revolution was broadcast on NPR and we SLEPT
THROUGH IT!
Meanwhile, our mothers are busy at the stove,
cooking CHAOS passed out free
at most GUILT-RIDDEN CHURCHES
in a pot of steaming social pollution
from which we eat nightly!

Bow your nappy heads and Pray
That you will NEVER be misunderstood
IF you are heard AT ALL!

People!! We are living in the age of the BLACK PLAGUE
A deadly diss-ease for which there is NO KNOWN CURE!

The sickness begins with a sudden fever
And is accompanied by the dropping off syllables of words
And an unquenchable need to get on welfare!
Or-Is it just a ploy
To distract us long enough
While the Oakland School Board Rifles thru our pockets
like a THIEF IN THE NIGHT
Just to get their paws on UNTAPPED FEDERAL $$

NOT so they can improve test scores,
But so they can keep up payments
on their TOWN CARS
and pay tuition for their kids to go to
PRIVATE SCHOOL!!!

WHA—?!? WHAT?!?! Lemme Go!!! This is an open mic!!!
Lemme Go!!!
I got my rights! I got my rights!

*While this poet gets arrested, we'll take the opportunity
and have a breif word from our sponsor...*

And now...Presenting exclusive scenes from one of the most highly anticipated films of the year!!!

From the people who brought you:

BEBE'S KIDS II: Horny Alone
UNCLE TOM'S CRACKHOUSE
and the Oscar-Winning SENSE & SENSIMILLA

comes...

William Shakespeare's
HAMBONE N' THE HOOD

25

HAMBONE:

You either is, or you ain't. That's what I'm talking about! Is it hype to stress over BULLSHIT, or get sick wid it and do a DRIVE-BY on them muthafuckas?!? I'm down wid givin up this bitch, this life, if that's what it take to end this madness that got fools straight up buggin'! I'm wid it, peep game…To take a dirt nap, or just bust some serious ZZZ's. Hell yeah, to chill. Dig: The dreams you have in the grave must be a bitch, you don't hear me. You just gon lie there and le life and time get ill and try to fade you? I ain't wid that! Nig-gahs go to the crossroads and neva come back. Maybe we ought to deal wid what's on earth now, rather than run from shit like a straight up mark!

SEE HAMBONE chill with his homeboy HORATIO!

HAMBONE:

Gimme dat skull, punk! (He grabs the skull and starts tripping!) Damn, Yoric! I knew this nigga, Horatio! This was my homie! He was a straight up fool! He had my back hella times and now its foul just to look at him! This was my dog, yo—back in the day we wuz hella tight! Wit his 'yo momma' jokes and shit…He had nig-gas **rollin!** Where your yo momma jokes ow, dog?

Yes! Run—Don't Walk to Dig
HAMBONE N' THE HOOD
Now Playing, Fool!

WE NOW RETURN YOU TO OUR REGULARLY SCHEDULED POEM ALREADY IN PROGRESS…
Our language, such as it is, is a colloquial gumbo.
A playful reinvention of old concepts. A mis-match of
various words and phrases taken from various places
      Just   Like   English
But, you say, we don't SPEAK English, well…

What is an English word?
Rodeo? Buffalo? Lariat? Pinto? Canyon? Cockroach?
<blockquote>all SPANISH!</blockquote>

What is an English word?
Waffle? Bedspread? Boss? Cookie? Hex? Landscape?
<blockquote>all DUTCH!</blockquote>

What is an English word?
Procrastination? Castle? Music? Dance? Crime? Prairie?
<blockquote>all FRENCH!</blockquote>

What is an ENGLISH word?
Delicatessen? Ecology? Dumb? Hamburger? Vampire? Check?
<blockquote>all GERMAN!</blockquote>

What is an ENGLISH word?
Tote? Banana? Banjo? Jumbo? Jukebox?
<blockquote>all AFRICAN!</blockquote>

What is an ENGLISH word? Ghetto? Shyster? Putz? Schlep?
Chutzpuh? Kosher?
<blockquote>all YIDDISH!</blockquote>

Which is a GERMAN-based language

So I ask you, What language do WE speak?

No—What language do YOU speak

CULTURE SHOCK NEWS SHOW (CSN)

Through its production company, Quilombo Enterprises ICM, *CSN* has been continuously broadcasting in the Bay Area, since 1992 at Peralta Community TV (PCTV) Laney College, Oakland, California. *CSN* has evolved over the past 10 years, from a studio based talk/interview show; to a poetry performance, documentary, social commentary, dance and music performance based news magazine. *CSN* has featured prominent local artists like, John Santos, Opal Palmer Adisa, and Piri Thomas. *CSN* recorded and broadcast a lecture by Dr. Cornel West called "The Souls of Black Folks; the video "La Promisa" about the annual celebration of St. Lazarus in Cuba; and the historical documentary "HMS Win-drush", the story of the first Jamaican immigrants to Great Britain in 1948. In the last few years in collaboration with the National Poetry Association, Inc. and its video archives promoted through Literary Television (LTV), CSN has emphasized performance poetry. Because of this association with the NPA/LTV and access to their video archive of over 500 cin(e) poems, prominent local Slam poets have been broadcast on my show, as have international video poet performances. **CSN's** mantra is "Changing the World through Poetry" because we believe poetry is the last refuge of the individual in our society today.

MISSION STATEMENT & VISION:
1) To provide a forum where the people of the world can express their thoughts and feelings about their vision for the 21st century.
2) To facilitate the integration of diverse cultures into the host country of their choice.
3) To provide a forum where conflicts resolution between and within cultures can take place.
4) To entertain and enlighten through poetry performance and individual creative expression.
5) To change the world through poetry.

The following is a transcript of one of my shows from 1993, which features interviews with eight individuals who comment on their Culture Shock experiences in America.

HOST-IAN MOORE:

Culture Shock is about the shock of cultures coming together in our world today. Culture Shock is the change that is thrust on someone before they've had time to fully absorb it and adjust. Culture Shock is living next door to someone whose language and ideas represent a challenge to our assumptions about who we think we are. We at Culture Shock want to stimulate your interests in all the people and ideas around you. Culture Shock intends to be a forum where people of the world can voice their thoughts and feelings about their vision of a multicultural society.

Hi, my name is Ian Moore. My guests today come from many different parts of the world. But they all have one thing in common, respect for each other's cultures. In this disillusioned and contentious world of ours today, this is a rare quality. So let us listen to their stories, and discover what it takes to really love thy neighbor.

PIRI THOMAS (WRITER & POET):

And we of the rainbow and we of all the colors must learn how now to unite. For they are truly the minority that breed name greed. Those demons that look like humans and they're really not. That bends their knees in prayer and mouths the words of Christ and brotherhood, peace on earth, and goodwill, and all of that Kau-Ka, and they know truly in their hearts that they are lying. Because while they are laughing and living well, Indian children, Black children, Red children, Yellow children, White children, children, children, children. Hey man, all kinds of children, are dying physically, mentally, immorally, hey and spiritually in broad daylight. I admire me, I'm a majority of one. I come to share, man.

TALIBAH TILLMAN (EDUCATOR-AFRO-AMERICAN)

In London, I felt very rich, very rich indeed; and especially with the Black Londoners. I even began to pick up their accent somewhat.

How ever, I found myself more welcome in certain places in Europe than I did in my own country.

HOST-IAN MOORE:

Did you get a sense of why that might have been?

TALIBAH TILLMAN:

Well you know, I believe that the truth is what sets one free. And I believe that in certain parts of Europe they actually admit and they Know the truth and they live the truth. They know from whence they have come. We all know. In America, they refuse to admit that everyone come from where—the African soil! Everyone, the first man and woman were of African descent. So every body is an extension of that. Well, in America, they have a problem with that. In Europe, especially in certain parts, they don't have a problem with it. They know it, they realize it, they admit it, and they live up to that.

ANNA CORTEZ (ENGINEER-EL SALVADOR):

Well, I think respect is definitely, I feel the clue and the key for solving the problems that we're facing right now as we speak. The racial disturbances that have occurred in the last year or so (Los Angeles-1992). It's not like they haven't been around, it's just that now they're more obvious. But I Think that respect of other individuals and their cultures is essential. As long as you see other cultures as down or below your culture, you will not have equality. And if you don't have equality, you don't have respect. That level playing field, I may say, need to be in place.

PHILLIP AUERBACH (PUBLISHER-JEWISH AMERICAN):

It's obvious that this is becoming a far more multicultural society moving away from the Euro-centric approach that we've traditionally had and moving more toward, I'm not sure what, perhaps an Asian approach or a Latin American approach. Or simply a greater awareness that there are other peoples out there and other ways of looking at things. So, in some ways, yes, I see definitely that there is more of a shifting of American ways of interacting with people. But

31

on the other hand, I don't see that there is going to be a radical shift in what defines Americans as a people because this is a very absorbing culture. It does not ask, as some countries do, that you abandon your culture and suppress it to become part of the American culture, as for example, France does. But it does say that you may retain your home culture, and still, when you interact in the main stream that you adapt certain ways of thinking, behaving, and operating. And that may shift to some extent. But ultimately, I don't think so. And that's largely because most immigrants come here for the very values that the United States embodies, which is freedom, initiative, being able to make it on your own. Independence, the achievement ethic, not being constrained by political systems, by religious systems, by political oppression of different kinds, whatever the case may be.

PAUL CHIDEYA (STUDENT-ZIMBABWE)

I see America, I think if you really work hard, you have a great opportunity and I want to do that. I'm going to work hard so that I can make my dream come true. And what I want to do, I can prosper in doing it.

CARLOS GONZALES-IRAGO (TEACHER-VENEZUELA)

Well, one of the things I think is that we should change our way of thinking and our ways about our culture and other people's cultures, because there is always this idea that you have to impose your culture on somebody else. You have to defend your own culture. It is true. You have your own culture and you are proud of it, and you feel that you are a part of it and in a way, you feel the connections with these people, even a spiritual connection with these people. And you have a common language, and you have foods, and you have traditional dances and things like that.

; kWhat I think is an excellent way of connecting with your own people. But in the same way, there are other ways to connect with people who are from different cultures. I have a tremendous experience in this country I like. I have met people from all over the world. People I would never imagine I would meet, like people from

India, people from Asia, Africa, Ethiopia, Somalia, every country in the world.

When you find a Third World person in this country, you immediately feel there's some kind of connection, and I think the connection is, that you are in a position where you cannot have cultural dominance and you are in a situation where you don't have the control. So you communicate openly and equally.

ELAINE PEACOCK (COLLEGE PROFESSOR):

Well, you see, I think before the term multiculturalism existed, there were always values such as tolerance, such as compassion, such as understanding, such as respect. And these were always there. These were already in existence, If we're talking about 'universal values'ind of timeless and ageless values. These were already in the book, and we already could have tried to meet the challenge of tolerance, of understanding, of respect, of justice, and all of those things. So I think we always had the opportunity. And multiculturalism doesn't give us a new opportunity. It doesn't necessarily answer questions that were not always problematic. It's very interesting to me that even within families, even an individual, and even you, Ian, and even I, are really kind of a culture. I mean you've got your personal culture. I have my personal culture and what we're often faced with is how to respect human individuality, which is like individual cultures in a sense. I mean I'm taking these unites and trying to compare them so that a Thai culture and a Russian culture is much like an individual called Ian, meeting an individual called Elaine. And so the question of how do we co-exist together as two individuals is one of how do I respect you? How do I see that you have a way of looking at the world that's different from my own. And what's important in both of these exchanges, and I'm not sure if multiculturalism resolves this question, is why I find it problematic. What I'm not sure that multiculturalism does, is that it heightens and confirms and reaffirms the respect for the individuality, if it doesn't suggest submerging something into a big mix.

This is how I read multiculturalism. Provide it doesn't say what you need to give up. And this is what you need to give up. And in coming together you have just submerged differences. Now what I'm interested in doing as an individual in this culture, to your culture, is not giving up my true nature. But meeting your true nature and having my true nature and your true nature meet each other. And we respect it, we tolerate it, we understand it, and that you retain your identity as Ian and I retain my identity as Elaine.

ERIC ORLANDER (JOURNALIST):

Jesse Jackson came here about three or four weeks ago and he gave a speech on the Berkeley campus and he said that the Bay Area, Berkeley specifically, was one of the most ethnically and culturally diverse places on the planet. And he has this traditional thing of how he says, "you know, the United States is not a melting pot, we're a tossed salad." And for evidence of this he says, "The Bay Area is perfect;" because he says, "we're all here. All of these different cultures, we have Latinos; we have Chinese, we have Mexicans, we have Africans, Puerto Ricans, Americans and etc. All of these different cultures are all here in one place. But we don't necessarily interact with each other. That's where the salad analogy comes in. You have the tomatoes and lettuce, but they don't necessarily blend into one as the melting pot theory goes. And living in Berkeley and living in the Bay Area, you really come to appreciate that, especially on campus. If you just take a stroll over to the campus around lunchtime on Sproul Plaza, you'll see the Blacks over here, the Chinese are over here, the Koreans are over here, and the Whites are everywhere else. Everyone is in his or her little corner. So growing up with this, you realize that, yes, in fact there are lots of different people in this world, in the Bay Area, in Berkeley. But we don't always interact as much as we probably should and that I believe is the source of a lot of the problems in our culture, in our world.

IAN MOORE (HOST):

We all experience Culture shock daily, although we sometimes don't recognize it. Sometimes it's as a result of moving to another country. Other times it's because of ethnic bigotry, which eats at the heart of all nations. But if we truly believe in freedom, we must demonstrate our belief by giving the opportunity to everybody to be heard. And more importantly, we must listen to them.

TALIBAH TILLMAN:
I'll start first with moving from the South to the West. One thing about the South, if it's racism you know it. It isn't hidden. It's there. I don't like you, I gotta work with you, I will, but you know we don't like each other. You are not as good as I, you know the White talking to the Black. Here it's [in California] very subtle and hidden, which makes it even more dangerous. It's, I like you in front of your face; I pretend to like you; I pretend that you're good; I pretend that you're as equal as I am. But behind the back, when we are meeting alone, I will stab you in the back. I noticed that right away. And anybody who comes from the South, who has been taught by black teachers, you recognize racism whether it's subtle, undercover, or whatever. Here I found that there is a lot of undercover racism. African Americans who were born here, however, in the West don't recognize it as readily as one who comes from the South.

IAN MOORE:
Why do you think that is?

TALIBAH TILLMAN:
Because they were taught by a mixture of teachers. And basically most of them were white, in most cases. Where we've come from, a background of all Black teachers, and Black teachers were the ones who taught you about yourself; who you were and what society was about; and how to look at racism, and what it is. Whereas here, they didn't talk about it. It was there, but the kid was supposed to think everybody loved him and everything was fine as long as you remained in your place.

IAN MOORE:
What did you like most about living in El Salvador?

ANNA CORTEZ:

Not experiencing Culture Shock. When you're in your own country, you don't think about your identity, because you live it everyday. You don't have to validate yourself or your culture everyday. There's no need to do that. So I miss the feeling of just being at home relaxed, not having to think or defend who you are or define who you are everyday.

PHILIP AUERBACH:

The Americans very much believe in taking the initiative and making things happen and creating their own destinies. And this idea of individuality and also initiative very much conflicts with the idea of consensus which is the way most other cultures operate. When I say most, I mean most non-Western, mostly European cultures operate, in that most people believe in resolving conflicts, resolving any kind of issue through the idea of talking, or coming to some kind of agreement, not necessarily by voting. When you vote, there's a majority and a minority. And the minority often feels angry or excluded or betrayed-sometimes betrayed-it depends on the issue. But they know they have to swallow their hurt and go along with what the majority wants because that's the definition of democracy. And certainly in a consensus, people come to understandings and it's more of a group decision.

PAUL CHIDEYA:

I've experienced Culture Shock because of cultural differences between California and Zimbabwe, where I'm from. In America, I have seen many important things I didn't expect and I didn't know that is taking place here. For example, in Zimbabwe, I think they are more family orientated than here in America. I'm not saying that America does not have that sense. For example, I'll tell you, when I came here, every since I came here, everyday, I can hear on the news that "oh this person has been murdered." But in Zimbabwe, you don't find that kind of thing. People are murdered, of course every year. But the rate is not as high as here in America. I think people murdered in America in one week they total to people murdered in my country for the whole year. We have seen the big difference in cultures. But one thing about the traditions of Zimbabwe, again I think it's kind of powerful people there afraid to murder because traditionally they are going to pay for it, besides being brought to court and sentenced by the judiciary. If you kill a person, especially among the Shona culture, there's a thing they name, which is a traditional way whereby if a person murders someone, they have to pay for it, maybe you die or the spirit comes down to you to haunt you for the rest of your life or it can haunt your family. It comes in different ways which is a powerful force.

IAN MOORE:
Is there anything else that you found different when you came to America that sort of shocked you, that you didn't expect?

PAUL CHIDEYA:
Well I didn't expect to see homeless people, people sleeping in the street, in bus stations. I was quite shocked when I saw that. I didn't expect to see that kind of thing. But like the buildings and the cities are just the same like in Zimbabwc.

IAN MOORE:
Coming to America, for you then, was a pretty traumatic experience.

CARLOS GONZALES-IRAGO:
Well, it wasn't as traumatic as the one I had in Spain. Because I was already a person with a lot of experience, when I came to America. I had been working in Venezuela as a Journalist for a long time, like five years, and I was already politically and psychologically a mature person. So I knew I could do some things, I knew I could learn this culture without forgetting my own, and using my own to get into this culture. But I understand for people who don't have a background, who don't have—like I'm a teacher in Junior High school, teaching teenagers—for people who don't have information. Culture Shock must be tremendous for those people, because you go from a home based culture to a culture where you don't even speak the

language of the people. And it's a culture that is very much imposed on you without-like you speak another language but it's not the language that people speak here. So you have to have real values, culturally, if you are to adapt successfully. And that's a problem I see with a culture. Cultures can live together, and can learn from each other. And I learned that. I think to learn the American culture has opened my eyes to a New World, different perspectives. I have also had the other perspective. So I have both, and I have more intellectual enrichment. So in that way it's good. I would like to go to India and learn all about the Indian culture, or go to Japan and learn Japanese. Because I think that's when you can open more your growth perspective of the world.

ELAINE PEACOCK:

My problem with Culture Shock is very profound, much more than I anticipated. You think when you move within the country of your birth, within national boundaries and borders, that you're gonna be O.K. That somehow you have been prepared and you've been equipped. I moved from Mississippi, from the rural South, from the deep South, and that's what Mississippi is. I moved to the Bay Area when I was in my late thirties. This was in the late eighties, and I found that I just wasn't prepared for the different quality of human relationships. As I mentioned earlier, this sense of responsibility that you have to each other and for each other, that was certainly lacking. But what seems to be most important is a sense of efficiency in a city. So a concern for efficiency as opposed to a concern for responsibility that you owe each other as members of a group or community or whatever, those are kind of conflicting to a certain extent. So my Culture Shock, I think really took place around issues of how to rearrange my emotions. What should I expect from people? I always thought that I could rely on people that I met with, whom I identified with, to give me their very best advice. Or they're very best feedback. And that it would somehow be not something necessarily to reinforce their own views. But somehow they would try to figure out, "well, what is it that she seems to need right now? Let me give her what I think she needs in order to sustain herself." And I didn't find that always to be the case. I found it interesting. Of course, it's caused me to grow up. Now I understand that one of the things that moving from a rural area to an urban area teaches you is a strange sort of self-sufficiency.

CARLOS GONZALES-IRAGO:

You can get to a point when you can say, well, this culture is right on this issue, and can enrich my own life this way. And this other culture can do this for me. In a way, in this country, it is really an intercultural mixture and is really wealthy in a sense because you have people from everywhere in the world. It's like sometimes I think, why not have a school of languages in Oakland, when you have people from every country you can imagine, Vietnam, India, Spain, Mexico, Portugal etc. You can have here the greatest teaching of many cultures, including the Anglo Saxon culture, besides Native American cultures. However, you don't see that. And this is unfortunate. Many people who come to America are faced with the reality of drowning their own cultures in the rush to become American as soon as possible. This robs both America and the individual of the richness that this country promises.

IAN MOORE:

Tell me three advantages that you could tell a person, to encourage them to become more aware of different cultures.

ERIC OLANDER:

This is specifically from the college level, because when you graduate from college, you're in the mind-set of getting a job. From learning another person's culture, that is, stepping out of your own and learning something that is completely foreign to you, that is for me to study African culture. It makes me far more marketable in the job market because I am now able to not only deal with the traditional client base, but I, for my employer, can expand. I can expand into the African market or I can expand into the American market where there is a large African community. You make yourself far more marketable business wise. Intellectually, you're also making yourself far more marketable because you now are open up to new ideas which can help you solve your own problems. By learning about Africa, I can learn a lot about myself. That is, by studying America's history and Western European history, colonial history in Africa, I learn about my own history.

PIRI THOMAS:

From that day on, it was mine, it was mine, it was mine. They plunged us into feeling inferiority complex picking out white as the national anthem of the world where white is right. And I have learned that it's not no longer, it's never ever been a matter of geographical locations of color or sex or sexual preferences, if you please, but rather a matter of human dignity. I am not a number. I was not born a criminal from my beautiful mother's womb. I was born like other children. But I kept repeating all these things over and over again. I'll probably be known as Peter the repeater. But I certainly believe that certain things bear repetition since there is somuch repetition of the indignity over and over again. No color was meant to be inferior. No more than any other color was meant to be superior. We are not minorities. In the dictionary it means less than. If anything at all, we are each one a majority of one similar to each other like fingerprints and cultures. So viva la difference man, let's learn from each other. Learn baby, not burn.

IAN MOORE:

We have seen how the experiences of different people from different parts of the world can make for interesting and valuable contributions to our understanding of life here in America. For many of you watching, this look into the lives of our guests may be the only opportunity you have to hear and feel the concerns of different people from different cultures. We at Culture Shock News Show want to stimulate your interest in all the people and ideas around you. Culture Shock intends to be a forum where the people of the world can express their thoughts and feelings about their vision of a multicultural society.

MARKET CULTURE
by John Seabrook

The culture of Marketing is part of the [aesthetic] of reality TV. The aesthetics of reality that people want to hear—people speaking the way they speak on the street, or they want to watch sports and they want to hear what the guys actually say in the huddle, or they want to hear Rappers rapping how they really rap and not how they rap for TV. A lot of people are fed up with the attempt to filter out by taste-makers and they say, "Just give me the real stuff. Give me what the real language is, and I'll be the one that decides whether it's coarse or not coarse."

So, on the one hand, it is culture. But, on the other hand, it's an advertisement for the CDs. That's who pays for it. The record companies pay for those videos to be made, or the artist's pay for them out of the money the record company gives to them. And the record company is putting them on MTV in order to sell CDs. That breakdown between culture and marketing is quite new, when you think how television was traditionally constructed. You had the advertisements, and then you had the programming, although in the very early days of television, it's true you often would have a Sponsor on the show to remind you that Lucky Strike or whoever it might be was bringing this to you. But at least there was a significant break.

Then, in the 1970s, 1980s, 1990s…there was this crunching together. There's another aspect of that closed feedback loop…The gist of the videos, especially in the rap videos…is full of gestures, secret language, and signals in clothing. MTV takes that from a very underground subculture, which, without MTV, would never really get very far beyond that little underground subculture. But MTV takes that and puts it on MTV and spreads it everywhere, so that the kids in Kansas and the kids in Los Angeles and the kids in Tokyo and the kids in London are all seeing this little underground subculture language. It's happening very quickly, and then they're starting to wear those clothes or make those gestures or use that slang. That is a very remarkable new thing. Another thing that's very important about

MTV is that it breaks down the time that it used to take for these things to filter out. By putting them in the street, it shows the filmmakers their ideas in the street after they put them on MTV—perhaps a matter of weeks—, which then further influences, their ideas in terms of what they do their next video as. So that feedback loop is very, very tight.

It does seem very suffocating. MTV does represent African-American and white culture side-by-side in a way that few networks do, where it's more either Black or White. And although on MTV you do see people of different races together and that's good, the versions of African-American and White life are so narrowly constrained in terms of what MTV chooses to show you about those lives, that in a way, it's not as diverse as it seems. It seems like a picture of diversity, but the reality of it is fairly homogenous.

And so when we talk about the feedback loops there, it's very clear that people are seeing what they think of as life on MTV. And then, they're going out and trying to live that life, which would be a cultural noncommercial version of that. But because what MTV shows you is very limited in terms of the choices that you can make, the life that you try to lead based on MTV becomes very sterile, homogenous and boring. And then all you have to do is watch more MTV, and the loop gets tighter and tighter.

There's also the point of the importance of visual information and reading things—reading purely visual information—and how that's different from a literary culture that is based on reading print. When you read and when you understand print, you do tend to make distinctions about, "Is the intent of this commercial, or is the intent of this somehow beyond commercialism? Is it cultural in a non-commercial sense?" And when you're reading literature, it's easier to make that distinction than when you're taking in visual images, because visual images can go both ways much more easily than words can go both ways.

[Yet] we all still crave the quiet, non-commercial spaces in our lives. We treasure them. And whether we're aware of it as adults or whether we just do it spontaneously as kids, there are still those distinctions made in everyone's life that this is all part of MTV and that this is not life.

If you think about the progress of MTV through the years, it's been to gradually push that boundary. The quiet, non-commercial space is shrunk more and more. Now kids' social life is made up of commercial culture to a very large degree, whether it's, "Oh, I see you're wearing Tommy Hilfiger," and "Why are you doing that and not wearing Polo?" Or, "Did you see the Limp Bizkit ad video on MTV?" These are the reference points. It's no longer, "Do you want to go down and see if we can see some turtles at the lake?" Those kinds of experiences are discouraged, partly because they're not as exciting and fun and not as many people engage in them, and also because you don't seen them on MTV.

> Hip hop slang
> Rubs dud-dud sounds.
> The music for whites that cannot dance
> And blacks that cannot sing.
> Them loaded down
> In oversized threads
> Ignorant of history and
> their place in the scheme.
> Them giant clothes hide them midget spirits
>
> Desperate for sight,
> A light in the world.
>
> *It's the poverty of plenty*
> *In the land of the brave*
> *Too fixed on the money*
> *When there are souls to be saved.*
>
> *It's the poverty of plenty*
> *Fooling all who seek truth?*
> *'Cause the thieves of the past*
> *Have just donned New boots.*

43

Oh the Hip Hop slangers,
What a joke to the real
All remembering a past they've never fulfilled.
They cry over scares that they've never had to shed,
While they climb on the backs of their brothers who
Bled for freedom and, justice and respect, for a truth,
Now lost in the smock of a glided punk's tooth.

It's the poverty of plenty
In the land of the brave
Too fixed on the money
When there are souls to be saved.

It's the poverty of plenty
Fooling all who seek truth?
'Cause the thieves of the past
Have just donned New boots.

So let them Hip Hop 'til the cows come home.
It can't feed their kids and it can't feed Their souls.
And one day they'll wake from a shattering dream
To realize they can't even HEAR

Let alone understand the word PEACE!

Kweku Dawkins

We come from a world where there was a sense of a high culture that was occupied by the few. Then, the mass culture was looking up to the high culture, and it hopefully filtered down in a trickle-down theory of culture.

That high culture has now been exposed as an elitist, narrowly focused culture of only a few privileged people, and that whole system of high and low has tended to fall apart. What's taken its place is this hierarchy of subculture and mainstream culture, where the subculture is on the top. And the subculture has integrity, because it has a reality. It's based on ethnic practices; or it's based on community values; it's based on specific neighborhood areas and the practices of those neighborhoods. And that gives those particular styles or ideas of motifs, whatever they maybe, an authenticity, and integrity. Then they are expanded and, through media, are made mainstream.

For a moment, the mainstream is refreshed and uplifted by those authentic sub cultural values. But then they're quickly mediated and become no longer sub cultural or no longer authentic. And that leads to the constant desire for more authenticity and more subculture. It becomes like a big strip mine, where you're just desperately feeding this ravening maw of mainstream culture with the more and more valuable, but increasingly rare, authentic culture that people crave.

Everyone who lives in a subculture, if they're truly deep in that subculture, might not have a whole lot of points of reference in common with another subculture. So they look to the mainstream culture for things in common, and the mainstream culture has the big blockbuster movies and Britney Spears. You can either like them or not like them. But you can be quite sure that if you express an opinion about one of those things, someone else will know what you're talking about.

But the opposite side of that dynamic is that, as everyone spends time in this mainstream culture where everything is false by definition and mediated almost into a homogenized state, you're driven, in turn, to desire that subculture, because you desire authenticity. You're sick of the mediated state of mainstream culture, where everything seems fake, and so you turn back to the subcultures in search of some reality, some authenticity. So the small grids and the big grids reinforce each other, and together make commercial culture, as we know it today.

In a crowded marketplace, where everyone is trying to be heard and where there's an amazing number of choices, the loudest, coarsest, most shocking voice does tend to be the one that at least grabs your attention for a moment. And since moments are the currency within which modern media trade, that's all that really matters.

> On the continent's shores
> They stand side by side
> Looking back on a heaven
> They stole from God's hide.

It's a myopic Utopia of the overfed
It's a myopic Utopia of the culturally dead.

In a world of diversity
Spanning the globe.
They want no part unless
It shares their own goals.
Of golden arches and neon beams
A cultural wasteland of corporate greed.

Stop the buying and count the cost
Stop the buying before we're all lost.

Though the first price of greed
Is a great cost to themselves, just
Look how they raised their children and Breed!
Their infants are drugged by TV's consumer wars
While their teens shoot each other
And are turned into whores.

It's a myopic Utopia of the overfed
It's a myopic Utopia of the culturally dead.

That this land once possessed
Great spirits-and a new art
And minds that re-wrote the
Visions of the heart,
Is still somewhere buried
In the core of this land
But needs love miners
To dig beneath the scam.

Stop the buying and count the cost
Stop the buying before we're all lost.

As a man of the land
It brings bitter tears
To see all God's abundance
Submerged beneath great fears.
For surely this bounty is sent as a test
To see if mankind can live at her best.

In this myopic Utopia of the overfed
It's time to feed others before we're
ALL dead!

Kweku Dawkins

I.C. MOORE

THE CULTURE OF IGNORANCE

Information is power and ignorance is king in a society where fear & hatred are the essential ingredients of an economy.

The Culture of Ignorance springs from the desire of the desperate to hold sway over the masses, thereby ignoring any pretensions to a sense of humanity. These "leaders" in turn replace their own humanity with material possessions.

The Culture of Ignorance is also a function of the ugly, in spirit and body, who desire to convert the world around them to their own disfigured view.

Such harsh perspectives come from a culture of ignorance that has devastated the life of this planet and its hoped-for promise of improvement. Who now cannot believe how significant the deaths of the Kennedy's-John & Robert, and Martin Luther King were! If they had lived, along with many others who died in the sixties during the Civil Rights era and the Vietnam War, America would be a very different place today and so would the world. It is not too bold a statement to say that the world would be a much fairer and safer place than it is today had those martyrs for humanity survived.

Unfortunately we are now consumed by the shadow of the ignorant. The dummying down process is in full swing, registering all information void, if it does not display the whip-hand of the sponsors selling mantra. Such dictates have entered the food chain of the masses of people, who continue to feed at the trough of poor quality and infections, believing that cheapness equals better!

We live in a world where the access to information, that can address most of our individuals' ills, is readily available. Yet we live in parallel with a populace that knows less than their parents, and is proud of the fact. If we lived in medieval times we would surely conclude that the majority of the populace, have been bewitched. That someone, or something has put a spell on people such that they refuse to take advantage of information provided freely, that would improve the quality of their lives now.

> It use to be a convenient stereotype to attribute the deception of 'working people' to the machinations of power brokers in smoky back rooms, and in the past that may have been the case. But we are faced today with a new phenomenon. The vast majority of people on this planet prefer to be ignorant. Even in the face of horrendous crimes done in their name!

Thought was never a very popular notion, even when it first reared its questioning head in the 16th Century and the Age of Reason. Today it is irrelevant to the circus and roulette wheel that have taken over the functions of arbiters in our, once hoped for, civil society. Our wise men and women, who traditionally had a special place in society, have been either bought off, or ignored. The only message of 'consciousness' today is from popular musicians, who have ceased being artists, and have become megaphones for disharmony and chaos, while collecting huge kick-backs from increasingly debt-ridden corporate conglomerations paralyzed by real originality.

> Ignorance is real. Ignorance is powerful, and the repetition of its message only serves to emphasize the actual devolution that is occurring in contemporary life, as we stride forward into a world where science and economics will make redundant the majority of humanity.

If there is a hope, and if hope still has a future, it is in the very nature of the human being. For this pathetic and dehumanizing situation has happen before. In fact it is in many ways the fundamental challenge that has created the dynamic for human existence. The threat of extinction has always brought out a super human effort to survive. Of course the nature of that survival has always been the question, and too much attention is paid to 'what will happen after the fall', rather than focusing on the eventuality!

> That change is in the air, cannot be denied, for inevitably the weakness of ignorance is its own worse enemy. Namely, it has no plan but to stay alive and perpetuate itself. Always open for the sucker punch, never protected, and profoundly stupid, all intelligent people know that ignorance can only feed on itself, and left alone will wither and die. AMEN.

I.C. MOORE

<u>INCIDENT</u>

Once riding in old Baltimore,
Heart-filled, head-filled with glee,
I saw a Baltimorean
Keep looking straight at me.

Now I was eight and very small,
And he was no whit bigger,
And so I smiled, but he poked out
His tongue, and called me, "Nigger."

I saw the whole of Baltimore
From May until December;
Of all the things that happened there
That's all that I remember.

Countee Cullen

I.C. MOORE

CULTURE OF WASTE
By Vance Packard

A Quality product, like a quality education and a quality lifestyle, use to be the goal of all societies that considered themselves civilized. Starting in the home and schools, quality took on the notion of godliness and goodness. It was the defining line of an existence that was all too often cut short by war, sickness and enslavement. Even during the history of individual and collective slavery, the beacon of liberation passed through those hallowed halls of quality, which presaged integrity and freedom.

Yet what now must the teachers and mentors of today generation tell their students. A reality, that will have to deal with the diminished resources of this planet along with a larger population. It is a reality that will have no sympathy for past hurts and repression's, for there is finiteness to all things. When we waste, we misuse the bounty of not only our own world, but that of our future world, most specifically, our children, that entity that we hold most true and dear to our own reason for living.

THE CITY OF THE FUTURE

In Cornucopia City all the buildings will be made of papier-mache. These houses can be torn down and rebuilt every spring and fall at housecleaning time. The motorcars of Cornucopia will be made of a lightweight plastic that develops fatigue and begins to melt if driven more than four thousand miles. Owners who turn in their old motor cars at the regular turn-in dates-New Year's, Easter, Independence Day, and Labor Day-will be rewarded with a one-hundred dollar United States Prosperity-Through-Growth Bond for each motorcar turned in. And a special additional bond will be awarded to those families able to turn in four or more motorcars at each disposal date.

One fourth of the factories of Cornucopia City will be located on the edge of a cliff, and the ends of their assembly lines can be swung to the front or rear doors depending upon the public demand for the product being produced.   When demand is slack, the end of the assembly line will be swung to the rear door and the output of refrigerators or other products will drop out of sight and go directly to their graveyard without first overwhelming the consumer market.

Every Monday, the people of Cornucopia City will stage a gala launching of a rocket into outer space at the local Air Force base. This is another of their contributions to national prosperity.   Eighteen subcontractors and prime contractors in the area will have made components for the rockets.   One officially stated objective of the space probing will be to report to the earth people what the backside of Neptune's moon looks like. Wednesday will be Navy Day. The Navy will send a surplus warship to the city dock. It will be filled with surplus playsuits, cake mix, vacuum cleaners, and trampolines that have been stockpiled at the local United States Department of commerce complex of warehouse for surplus products. The ship will go thirty miles out to sea, where the crew will sink it from a safe distance.

As a peek in on this Cornucopia City of the future, we learn that the big, heartening news of the week is the Guild of Appliance Repair Artists has passed a resolution declaring it unpatriotic for any member even to look inside an ailing appliance that is more than two years old.

The heart of Cornucopia City will be occupied by a titanic push-button super mart built to simulate a fairyland. This is where all the people spend many happy hours a week strolling and buying to their heart's content. In this paradise of high-velocity selling, there are no jangling cash registers to disrupt the holiday mood.   Instead, the shopping couples—with their five children trailing behind, each pushing his own shopping cart—gaily wave their lifetime electronic credit cards in front of a recording eye. Each child has his own card, which was issued to him/her at birth.

Conveniently located throughout the mart are receptacles where the people can dispose of the old-fashioned product they bought on a previous shopping designed sign by a receptacle reads: "throw your old watches here!" Cornucopia City's marvelous mart is open around the clock, Sundays included. For the Sunday shoppers who had developed a churchgoing habit in earlier years, there is a little chapel available for meditation in one of the side alcoves.

HEDONISM FOR THE MASSES

In the play "Raisin in the Sun", the son imbued with modern ideas voiced a lament that would delight most marketers. He cried:

"I want so many things, it drives me crazy…Money is life!"

His old-fashioned mother, sad and perplexed, replied: "You can't be satisfied just to be proud…How different we've become!"

The [consumer] marketers of the United States, in addition to developing specific strategies for moving goods, [have] developed an over-all strategy that would make all the others more effective. They [have] generated a love for possessions and a zest for finding momentary pleasures [in the products themselves]. They [have] encouraged Americans (and are now working on the global market) to break our of their old-fashioned inhibitions and to learn to live it up. All this, it was hope [and now come to pass] would produce a permissive mood for carefree buying.

Americans traditionally have liked to think of themselves as a frugal, hard-working, God-fearing people making sacrifices for their long haul. They have exalted such maxims of Ben Franklin as: "A man may, if he knows not how to save as he gets, keep his nose to the grindstone."

The settlers struggling to convert forest and prairie into a national homeland esteemed Puritanical traits necessary to survival. By the nineteenth century, however, a flamboyant streak was beginning to emerge clearly in the American character. Emerson observed that Americans, unlike Europeans, exhibited "an uncalculated, headlong expenditure."

As more and more Americans found themselves living in metropolitan areas, hedonism as a guiding philosophy of life gained more and more disciples. People [have] sought possessions more than formerly in emulation of, or competition with, their neighbors…

****

The central challenge of America today, and increasingly the rest of the world, is that we must learn to live with our abundance without being forced to impoverish our spirits by surrounding ourselves with more than we need, and being intoxicated with our success.

THE ICE AGE

The Cultural wasteland
Of our New World is
Cluttered with everything
We can eat, wear or screw.
A testament to our devolution!

LET GO
The pipe dreams of hope,
And be true to your
Deluded self!

RE-CAPTURE
The haunting tremors your spirit
Huddled behind the cut-out images
Of tomorrows call to arms.

FIND
A better job
Than the wail of pain seeking death comforts,
Frozen In the substance of your fears.

BREAK
The silent tundra of
Your heart's pitying alibi and

ACCEPT
Love's brotherhood of sharing GRACE!

Yes you...
    Yes you...
        Yes YOU,
            O Bohemian of the Ice Age!

Kweku Dawkins

I.C. MOORE

THE CULTURE OF WAR

The Culture of War is the currency of our species. The lie we hide behind as our tool for progress and the civilizing of mankind. It is the catalyst that propels our youth to die in the flames of heroic redundancy, while the parades of carnage continue to march through our history books.

> The Culture of War is the largest economic industry in the world consuming a third of the world's resources. One year's military budget for the world would feed everyone in the world for over 10 years.

The Culture of War is the root of the evil that mankind has invented for his distraction from the real challenge of human kind-to find spiritual and material harmony.

> As we emerge from the 20th century, a century that has seen the death and destruction of more human beings than at any other time in history, we seem not to have learned the lesson that violence begets violence, and that no amount of death will every create life.

But of course in many ways The Culture of War has not been about rightness, but about the desire of the few to dominate the many. It has been stated that war is the result of economic conflict aggravated by class conflict. And we can see how our world has become dominated by fewer and fewer people, while the majority of people have less and less control over their own lives.

> The Culture of War then becomes a reflection of that few holding onto their power, while the majority of humanity fight amongst itself over what is left.

The Culture of War is the psychology that we believe there is no alternative to war; that everything of value can only be achieved by conflict and competition; that human kind is naturally violent and the most violent amongst us should be indulged. Such is the lesson of humanity's history, and such is the nature of our societies, which have codified war and violence into our daily lives.

> The majority of our laws are designed around the idea of punishing the violent offender. Damage to property is on the top of that list. In recent years the all out assault to punish and incarcerate our youth has reflected the natural extension of this psychology.

Yet at the same time our business leaders dangle before these same youth, the temptations of products, attitudes, wealth and fame.
It is assumed apparently, that teenagers going through puberty and identity development should already have the experience and self control to withstand the unprecedented manipulation of their desires and feelings by corporate conglomerates, who are the very entities that support the laws that punish these same youth for their 'excesses'!

> The dichotomy, if not out right complicity, is chilling in its symmetry. At the beginning of the 20th century, our youth were trained as cannon fodder for the guns of our nation's armies. At the beginning of the 21st century our youth are cannon fodder for our consumer wars. Consume or die, is the message from our governments today!

The question needs to be asked, for we keep hiding from any sense of truth or honestly in this regard: What is the reason for a unique individual life, when so much of that existence is determined by others whose sole interest is to make money off their labor?

> If we are to change the culture of war, we must first challenge it within ourselves. We should wish to

ensure that nothing we do passes on the belief that violence achieves any positive results. We should remove our selves as much as possible from the intake of violent ideas: turn off the TV, refuse to buy guns, speak out against violence whenever it raises its insidious head at the dinning table of our cultural feasting. We should do these things as a part of our diet of healthy living, removing in stages the bad habits of laziness and self-indulgence that have allowed the virus of violence to become an accepted part of our being. For ultimately the profound weakness of violence is that it turns on itself and does far more damage to the one carrying the poison than to anyone else.

I.C. MOORE

THE CULTURE OF ACCEPTANCE
by Elie Wiesel

Why are people mistrustful of foreigners? Why do they hold them at arm's length?

A foreigner represents the unexpected, therefore he is a burden. You might say he came out of nowhere, and usurped someone else's place if not his life. He is shrouded in mystery, indefinable in his solitude. He lunges into a world that was there before he was, and which had no need of him. He arouses fear as much as he himself fears.

People are afraid of foreigners; there is no denying it. A foreigner conjures up the unknown, the forbidden. Who knows what he is doing on the sly. Perhaps he is cooking up plots and intrigues.

The foreigner represents something that we are not. He is different. He is an emissary of unknown, hostile powers. He is the vagabond in search of a resting place, the noisy Bohemian with a crowd of ragged children trailing behind him, the fugitive unjustly pursed by the law, the hungry beggar. He is the one nobody loves or welcomes, for whom scarcely any sympathy or compassion is felt. He is someone with whom we will never consent to identify ourselves.

The fear, which the foreigner inspires in us, causes us to see something in him, which calls into question our own role in society. Looking at him I realize that, like him, I am a foreigner in someone else's eyes. To that person, I am someone who arouses fear. On a human scale, this could mean that we are all foreigners. What if the other person was me? The truth is that he is. Or rather, it behooves me to act as if he were.

It is not because I have a home, a job, and a family that I am less foreign than the foreigner. It takes little for someone to be uprooted, for the satisfied, happy man to lose his place in the sun. My generation has seen just how unstable everything is and how vulnerable people are.

When destiny winked its eye, in the space of a day, the rich lost their treasures, men of status lost their friends, and thinkers lost their bearings. Suddenly, they found themselves deprived of their most basic rights.

France repudiated its Jews just as Hungary did. Military medals, aristocratic titles, social status, nothing counted any more. All it took was a decree, the stroke of a pen, and old families who had been living in supposedly civilized countries for centuries found themselves treated like foreigners and intruders.

It is enough for someone to treat me like a foreigner for me to be one. If I am excluded, it is because someone has pushed me out. Therefore, it is my fault, too, if the other person is excluded, that is to say deprived of a feeling of security and of belonging, of a sense of identity. For it is up to me whether someone feels at home or not in our common world, and whether he feels tranquil or anxious when he looks around him.

Since I am responsible for the other person being alienated or otherwise, just as I am responsible for his freedom, I must do everything in my power not to betray myself by betraying him. I must see in him my likeness, rather than a suspicious-looking stranger, so that our relationship can take on a human character. I live like him and I shall die like him. The same threats hang over us while we sleep. We cry out for rain or for love with the same voice. Despite appearances, despite the differences, the fate of people everywhere is the same.

Our passage on this Earth is part of a picture that transcends us. Is mine any more important than the other person's? Do I have a higher mission than he? No matter where he comes from, the foreigner is close to me. He conjures up visions of a world, which offers itself to us as a place to live in, enrich, and make fertile.

I remember that, as a child, I used to wait impatiently and lovingly for the unknown visitor to arrive. I waited for him so that I could make him talk and also so that I could dream. I was grateful for his presence. I shall never forget the hours I spent with strangers during my childhood. Some of them told me happy or sad stories. Others told me about faraway countries, inspired sages, or adventurers looking to put themselves to some sacred test. In my head I followed them, spellbound.

Their lives seemed so much more exciting than mine. I would have given anything to be like them, free as the wind and the night shadows. Yet most of them were beggars with no name and nowhere to go.

What attracted me to them was that they came from somewhere else. This is because, in the Jewish tradition from which I draw my inspiration, any foreigner might be a sage in disguise, perhaps even the prophet Elijah himself. Or he might be a righteous man in exile, and therefore cloaked in anonymity. To offend him would be to risk damnation. That used to be my attitude toward foreigners.

And now? I am older now. Am I any less romantic? Less optimistic perhaps. If I still respect the foreigner, it is for more concrete reasons. It is to let him know my solidarity with him as a human being, and my good faith as a human being.

Torn apart from his family, environment, and ethnic or national culture, he has rights over me, for legally he has no rights. I am his hope. To refuse him this hope would be to shirk my obligations as a man.

That is why I am in favor of welcoming as many foreigners as generously as possible. Whoever needs a refuge must feel welcome wherever I am. If he is a foreigner in my country, then I will be one too.

I.C. MOORE

THE CULTURE OF THE FUTURE

The Culture of the future is often no more than the culture of the past projected onto the future. Looking at life through the rear view mirror, is the expectation of most of us, desperate as we are to divine 'what will happen tomorrow?'

Yet the Culture of the Future is a separate reality that offers us the opportunity to reshape our lives in a new dimension of consciousness. Just take for example any change that has manifested itself through a previous action, or inaction! There was not only a causal effect in the effort expressed, but also a focused desire that willed the event, or non-event to happen. This is why the expression "a self fulfilling prophecy" has become such a acknowledged reality in the actualizing of our lives.

The Culture of the Future also requires that we face the challenges of our lives and our world with a courage that has been sadly lacking in the past. Complacency and selfish conceit have for too long been the dominant obsessions ruling the behavior of our leaders and us.

We are beginning to realize that there is a finite nature to the resources, and although science and engineering are constantly coming up with new ways to save time and effort, its in the social interaction of people to people that we require the greatest amount of tolerance and development.

We live constantly in a globally conscious environment, yet we still know so little about our next door neighbor. We are global only to the degree that we are consumer cannon-fodder for debit ridden companies churning out products that are designed to self-destruct in time for

the next round of empty, useless products, perpetuating
a process that has no end but to recycle vacuous things!

This process traps us in the slavery to economics based on the Old World Order of scarcity and want. In today's world of exploration and scientific creations, there is no scarcity in that old way. There is just a distribution problem. A minority, who control the most essential resources and manufacturing processes, due in large part through family lineage, elitist politics and criminal monopolies, are determined to keep the majority of the planet's inhabitants shackled to the additions of the past and their own material benefit.

Yet such has been the nature of this human experiment
on this planet since the beginning of time. Why change
you ask? Have we not seen how some have risen above
their social conditioning and advanced us all! And
haven't we evolved to limit the awesome power of the
tyrants of this world? I, myself have to acknowledge,
as I sit in comfort and security writing this book, that I
would have been killed long ago if the same forces of
the past held sway today. For a man born poor, I have
been able to travel the world, get a solid education, and
provide for my family in a secure and comfortable way.
Such realities say a lot about the world we live in today.

But can it be better? Yes it can and should be better! Particularly for those whose only sin was that they were born in a time and place when the devastation to their lands, was committed before their time. They who now are enslaved by the sons and daughters of the conquerors, who live in material comfort today. We live in a sorely unequal world, which has been created not invented. One of the aspect of globalizations is that this reality will become more pronounced.

Consumers now have more power than the global
corporations. More and more people around the world
realize the vulnerability of corporate power and we are

going to see more and more power exerted by the working people around the world.

The Culture of the Future will visit onto the sons and the daughters, the sins of their fathers and mothers. This we are seeing already. The extent of this payback, like the duality of good and bad will be proportionate to the actions-good or evil—that were perpetrated onto the world. This will be so, not because of some divine plan, but because the evil that men do lives after them and is part of the belief system that these perpetrators live by. The oppressor ultimately oppresses himself through denial of his own humanity!

Meanwhile those of us, who pursue the connecting spirit of humanity's love, will carry both the weight of these past sins and the challenge of establishing a new humanity. But just as evil fortune multiplies, good fortune (positive outlook) is exponential.

Happy the man
And happy he alone
He who can call this day his own
He who secure within
Can say tomorrow do thy worst
For I have lived today!

HENRY FIELDING

71

THE HEAVEN OF HOPE

This is the time of breathing money
And stapling dreams to the underside of experiences beckoning call.

For such moments flash by so quickly we fail to enjoy our failures
To live in the world of our sores crawling from beneath
Our sorry state of learning.
The daylight air catapults me through base anxieties, transforming
Before my eyes the jealousies of success
Pinned to the brow of my longed for escape.

Here in the heaven of hope.

Kweku Dawkins

AMERICA-CRY FREEDOM

A friend, who recently visited me from England confessed that he couldn't understand all this talk about an American Dream? He'd been in the country for a month and had found nobody who could satisfactorily explain to him this dynamic for dreaming in any logical language. It was he said like, some ethereal spirit that everyone is connected to yet nobody could rely on. For a pragmatic people it seemed to spit in the eye of everything American!

After twenty years of living in America, I too cannot put my finger on the pulse that captivates all who live in the dream of America. True, I've lived in California, for the majority of that time, and they say you lose one percentage point of your IQ, for every year that you live in La La land? But that notwithstanding, there is certainly a mystery to the bludgeoning materialism alongside the undaunted optimism that vibrates through all those who are consumed by this land.

When I stepped off the plane, twenty years ago into the sunshine of California's Mediterranean climate I believed that those warming currents would be sufficient to christen me with a new life of good fortune. But I soon found, to my disappointment, that the natives were not stimulated by the beautiful weather to be necessarily positive or even happy. One is constantly reminded of the adage that "travel broadens the mind', but for native people, whatever their stripes, they are forever crying about what they don't have, blind to what is before them.

My first misfortune was within my wife's family. My first wife, who I met on a whirlwind trip to the states in 1979, had an exuberance and beauty that had enthralled me within a day of meeting her, so much so that I left the country a married man. Two years later I staggered into this new environment, depleted of options in London, England, but apprehensive about the U. S of A being the best place for me to lick my wounds. But the weather was great, and it was initially my saving grace. So I immersed myself into its radiant environment, hopeful that this New World would be made real through the sympathy and compassion of my new family.

But this was not to be. I never fully appreciated the evil of racism until I was exposed to it's diseased underbelly. The popular lie perpetuated by black and white pundits of social order today is that everyone should be held responsible for their own actions, and that past events are just that—in the past! But we human beings are not so simple. Self-delusion is one of our greatest assets, and the past is a very living reality to those grasping for hope. Sometimes the association with mis-fortune through repetitions of pejorative language is more powerful than the real thing! This institutionalized attitude, in time, instills a deep psyche damage that is unreachable by any healing balm.

There was the fact that my wife's mother was mad. Not weirdly mad, pulling funning faces and burning her clothes in the fire mad, but a deeply disturbed madness that comes from years of denigration and heartache, and the inability to be free of her skin color. She was diseased by her feelings of failure and love-lessness, despite being a beautiful woman with intelligence to spare. This is not an unusual tale from the Heart(less) land of America. But what distinguished it was the callousness of her children.

Though her children escaped the awfulness of the color line, they showed her no sympathy for the pains she'd had to endure, or the terrors of raising five children alone. I don't believe anyone of her children had to face any real racial discrimination.

Oakland, California has had its share of racial strife. The Black Panthers-who were either bilking the local black businesses out of money "for the revolution" or performing sensational 'street theater' for the media, notwithstanding. There has never been a race riot in Oakland, even as other cities have burned and gored themselves on self-hatred and revenge.

Yet my wife and her siblings all carried slave ships in their shoes. It was as if certain words and attitudes set off in them a genetic psychosis completely outside of their control. My wife, who was the second eldest of the five, would withdraw into herself, at moments of dislocation, burrowing into a hole of unreach-able pity. Her next sibling, 6 years her junior, when vulnerable would react violently, both physically and mentally. I never realized how much I could hate someone until she kicked my wife and I out of her apartment a week before we were due to leave, anyway, all because I'd sat on her precious sofa!

The fourth child, a boy, was a completely indulgent wastrel, forever getting into trouble and having his sisters bale him out. And the youngest was the antipathy of the lot of them. A sweet nymph-like child who was the love-glue that all families should have, but who was so damaged by the surrounding malaise she barely stumbled through school, and was thankful to be married off early. The eldest sister had been abandoned years before, over a spate with the mother. And although none of her kids had anything to do with the spate, they enforced the ostracizing of their sister for fear of stirring the wrath of the mother.

Black, had never been a term I used towards another human being until I came to America. I was well aware of its use as a political term, in the literature of Black America from the 60's and 70's. And I'd come face to face with it during my meetings with black Americans while traveling through Europe. I always thought of the term as a Band-Aid to cover the festering sores of racism. Consequently, I was totally unprepared for the brutal hegemony of the term, as it referred to all people of color. Like the cultural hegemony of white America!

Black America believes they lead the world in racial superiority through their suffering and struggles. This view is enhanced by a myopic consciousness, which sees the struggles of the rest of the world only through their own eyes? On the one hand Blacks identify themselves daily by their skin color as different from whites, claiming a special moral credibility. Yet to each other, they've personified their self-hate to such a degree that communications have become an elaborate dozen's game filled with all the bitterness of the sport while devoid of any of the love! Meanwhile, whites moving around the edges of this pariah sub-culture, marketing the 'hip-ness' and accept 'without doubt' their natural superiority?

But, America is a conundrum for just as quickly as the blood boils to repel such chronic dichotomies, one is presented with the contrary position of acceptance. Not the acceptance of shared ideas that reach an apex of mutual disagreement through discussion and dissent. But the acceptance of philosophic indifference! The subject is changed. Materialistic endeavors fill up the pregnant pauses.

Sports-and the intellectual pursuit for a touchdown or home run-consume the brain cells and pumps the blood vessels with fire and brimstone. And then the question is asked. 'Why do you hold such contrary beliefs?' And without a breath, the dismissal, 'everyone loves football! Are you an alien or something?' The dictatorship of the majority-let us pray?

"But I like football," I say, "I just appreciate it for being a war game and not a sport"

"Well, I guess you never played the game, so how can YOU understand!" responds my Inquisitor.

"I don't have to be hit by a 6'8" defensive tackle to know that my body is not made for such violence", I reply.

But before the dialog can really get going-I'm always playing the Devils Advocate to provoke a discussion (can I help it if I was born to argue?). The subject is changed. My host walks out of the room, and I'm left alone with the TV blaring its testosterone triumph to consumerism.

Alexis de Tocqueville, claimed in *Democracy in America* "...that in no country in the civilized world is less attention paid to philosophy than in the United States." He goes on to add "...each American appeals only to the individual effort of his own understanding" The reality of such a profound statement is difficult to absorb for a someone like me from the 'Old World', where tradition and history are burned into the brain from an early age; a culture where the dialectic of class and worthiness that fixes one into a past, present and future, yoked to a societal identity and responsibility.

But Tocqueville, it must be remembered argued for the establishment of a monarchy, and his criticism was not so much anti-American, as anti democracies. Yet even this disclaimer cannot hide the dearth of discussion in contemporary America about anything to do with the institutions of government that guide and control the lives of this nation's people.

Fidel Castro of Cuba claims that 'Democracy in America is the freedom to go fishing on election day', and given the paltry turn outs of voters for civic society maybe we should all go fishing and drop the catch at the door of our representatives!

And what is this thing with fishing anyway. I'm prejudiced because I like fish as fish, not as sport. The thought of spending hours and hours looking at the bobbling motions of gut wire, surrounded by wriggling termites, while the full glare of bitterly cold nights forces you to intoxicate yourself to keep warm. Just to entrap pea brained fish, as mark of some machismo, seems pointless to say the least.

Every American male that I know goes fishing. And the few adventures I've been on reminded me of Mark Twain's comment about golf, "Its a waste of a good walk" In this case it's a waste of a good nature hike, an opportunity to really become one with nature, not just poach off of it!

I speculate that individuals who commune with nature, in that manner, and see themselves as a part of the 'big picture' rather than the 'master of the universe', would in turn develop some inner peace, particularly from the hectic tension filled worlds that they escape to come to these 'nature environments'. But here again I'm wrong. The true American individual does not let the immensity of the natural world change him or her. No! It is nature that must change to accommodate God's gift to the earth. The American colossus of manifest destiny! Now there's a true philosophy of the American way of life!

What I've had to admit too during my sojourn in this land of discoveries is that there are no absolutes. There are no traditions to hold onto, nor customs to live up too. There is, particularly in California, nothing to live for but yourself or what monopolizes your time. The sheer range of distractions...ops...I mean interests, are so staggering in their choices and absorption that to be born into this environment is simply a kaleidoscope of opportunities.

When I think back to the grinding misery I endured in London and Aberdeen. Where the price of a pint of beer and begging for a cigarette was my daily dream. It seems immoral to be now able to buy a six-pack of beer for the same price it cost me to buy a pint! And I guess that's what sustained my outrage and culture shock, when I first came to America. The immorality of such comfortable living! I have to admit to being intimidated by luxury!

Having only seen it from afar and always associating it with the 'privileged' I convinced myself that nothing good could ever come from living so well? Of course it was part of the bandaging process I used to insulate my damaged psyche from the pain of seeing myself as one of the lesser human kind; the human kind who is told that they can never rise above their station in life to which they were born; the human kind that lives on lies that disconnect the human from the self. And what does America say to all of this Hamlet-like self-doubt? "Shut the fuck up and eat!!" Comforting words indeed. But like the humor of this land, which took me some time to adjust too, because of its directness and absence of irony. I had to accept that living in America is a very very simple process. Just get up off your ass and do what you're here to do! And if you don't want to get up off your ass, don't! There will always be plenty of people out there in media land vying for your attention and entertainment dollars. So if you don't like what's on TV turn it off and go bungie jumping or something. And, of course, when all else fails you can always go shopping, which is not only the best in the world, because of the selection, but if you don't like what your bought you can take it back. Try doing that in Harrods of London?

What I've had to accept most profoundly about myself during my learning experience in America is that I'm a snob. Not a snob, who drinks the right wines, belongs to a selective club or has friends in high places, but a more insidious kind of snob. The kind of snob that hides behind the shackles of poor birth in a powerful country, and believes their inheritance endows them with superiority over the rest of the world; the kind of snob with the fatal malaise of the imperialist, who lives by proxy and is disconnected from the larger world's humanity.

Like many English people before me who have come to America, I was guilty of assuming that America was just another colony of 'Rule Britannia'. The overwhelming flattery I received because of my English accent confirmed in my own mind that I was on a divine mission to raise the consciousness of my colonial brothers and sisters to the true heights of British culture?

Such cultural bigotry is often the crutch, I think, all people adrift in a new culture cling to in order to make sense out of that new environment. But Patriotism, they say, is the 'last refuge of the scoundrel' and when it is used purely as a cloak to separate the individual from the light of truth, then we all have to second guess ourselves.

Traveling does that for the individual. For me it continually makes me ask the question: "What is happening here, and in what context is it happening?" For there is truly no A typical American, some cookie cutter identity flooding the airways, any more than there is a typical African or typical German. There are of course categories of demographics for economic units, but when was the last time you saw a supply and demand curve walking down the street?

In all seriousness though, perhaps we take things too serious. That's what a snob does. And what is most redundant for a lower class snob who spends his time being haughty over the cultural idiosynchrocises of others, is that it doesn't mean shit! He or she has no way of affecting anything at a higher level let alone at his or her own level with that attitude. What the cultural snob is left with however, and plenty of it, is misery, disappointment and abandonment.

But it must also be stated that there is always a room for more dialog within the American cultural experiment. As is taught in the history books, America is an unfinished Democracy. It has had some profound problems in its history and yet has faced more of them than nearly every other country in the world.

There are nevertheless still deep scares and painful legacies from those actions. But again compared to what? American politicians maybe some of the least inspired statesmen in the world, yet their pragmatism and optimism continues to defy doom and gloom social theorists.

This returns us to the question of what is the American dream. For all the pragmatic underpinnings of this society, the greatest force is that of optimism. An almost mystic-like feeling that grips everyone who comes to this land. The feeling intoxicates immigrants and

unfortunately they pay the price in many cases by working low paid
and slavish jobs. But there is always the hope. That feeling that if you
really do what you should be doing, you will go as far as your talents
will take you. Again, try that in Europe, Africa or Asia?

In conclusion, it has to be acknowledged that no society regardless
of its power and sophistication can sustain the ravages of time without
a healthy and vibrant dialog between its people about the substances of
its civic institutions, and its individual and collective commitment to
each other. Democracy, for all its shortcomings concerning dilution
and deflection of power, is our most powerful organ only when it is
exercised vigorously. When left to glory seekers and the expediency
of commerce we mortgage our souls to the marketplace and our
children's futures to the pocketbooks of greedy people.

"Everything may change in this disillusioned world of ours",
preached Marc Chagall "except the heart, and man's search for the
divine." And if we are to reach the heights of that search, within and
outside of ourselves, we need first to realize that listening to the
stranger across the table from each of us crosses the first bridge.
Realizing that we are often strangers to ourselves hiding behind flags
and symbols, which were invented to divide us as human beings. The
world is too old to look back now to some imagined golden age when
'things were better'. Like moving to a new country, the immigrant and
the native must accept that they have an opportunity to forge a new
future today; we cannot unravel history with words, or the absence of
love. We only have a future that has learned from the past and
continues to feed into the human desire to manifest the divine in
everyone's life here on this earth at this time.

The American dream finally for me is summed up in the one word-
joy. Not the joy that finds itself burying its head in the sand of
indifference to the responsibilities of freedom, nor popular culture's
chorus of the poverty of plenty, where people know the price of
everything and the value of nothing. It is the joy of knowing that there
is an opportunity in this society for me to exercise my dream of life,
liberty and the pursuit of happiness. No other nation dares state such a
declaration in its constitution and rights for its people! And although
that statement does not and has not applied to all its citizens in the

history of the United States up to today. It is a statement that is written down, and like the abolition of slavery, can and will be realized. There is a joy in the sheer audacity of the American dream, for its dreamy hope in the face of such pragmatic realities. And when it is accepted for the challenge that it represents; it is a joy that will propel even the most hardened grouch into a happy fellow. But don't take my word for it-try it yourself!

LET AMERICA BE AMERICA AGAIN
by Langston Hughes

Let America be America again.
Let it be the dream it used to be.
Let it be the pioneer on the plain
Seeking a home where he himself is free.

America never was America to me

Let America be the dream the dreamers dreamed—
Let it be that great strong land of love
Where never kings connive nor tyrants scheme
That any man be crushed by one above.

It never was America to me

O, let my land be a land where Liberty
Is crowned with no false patriotic wreath,
But opportunity is real, and life is free,
Equality is in the air that we breathe.

There's never been equality for me,
Nor freedom in this "homeland of the free."
Say who are you that mumbles in the dark?
And who are you that draws your veil
across the stars?

I am the poor white, fooled and pushed apart,
I am the Negro bearing slavery's scars.
I am the red man driven from the land,
I am the immigrant clutching the hope I seek—
And finding only the same old stupid plan
Of dog eat dog, of mighty crush the weak.

I am the young man, full of strength and hope,
Tangled in that ancient endless chain
Of profit, power, gain, of grab the land!
Of grab the gold! Of grab the ways of satisfying need!
Of work the men! Of take the pay!
Of owning everything for one's own greed!

> I am the farmer, bondsman to the soil.
> I am the worker sold to the machine.
> I am the Negro, servant to you all.
> I am the people, worried, hungry, mean—
> Hungry yet today despite the dream.
> Beaten yet today—O, Pioneer!
> I am the one who never got ahead,
> The poorest worker bartered throughout the years.

Yet I'm the one who dreamt our basic dream
In that Old World while still a serf of kings,
Who dreamt a dream so strong, so brave, so true,
That even yet its mighty daring sings
In every brick and stone, in every furrow turned
That's made America the land it has become.
O, I'm the man who sailed those early seas
In search of what I meant to be my home—

> For I'm the one who left dark Ireland's shore,
> And Poland's plain, and England's grassy lea,
> And torn from Black Africa's strand I came
> To build a "homeland of the free."

The Free?

A dream—still beckoning to me!

O, let America be America again—
The land that never has been yet—

And yet must be—
The land where every man is free.
The land that's mine
The poor man's, Indian's, Negro's, Me—
Who made America,
Whose sweat and blood, whose faith and pain,
Whose hand at the foundry, whose plow in the rain,
Must bring back our mighty dream again.

> Sure, call me any ugly name you choose—
> The steel of freedom does not stain.
> From those who live like leeches on the people's lives,
> We must take back our land again.
> America!
> O, yes
> I say it plain,

AMERICA, NEVER WAS AMERICA TO ME

> We, the people, must redeem
> Our lands, the mines, the plants, and the rivers
> The mountains and the endless plain—
> All, all the stretch of these great green states—
> And make America again!

For a catalog of Quilombo ICM products including:

Culture Shock News Show programs,
Great Black Inventor Educational Cards and T-shirts,
Great Black Innovator & the Problem Solving Process Poetry videos:
Langston Hughes' Let America be America Again & Freedoms Plow
Ebonic Plague-Slam poetry from James Cagney
West Oakland Senior Citizen's Oral Project
The Souls of Black Folks-W.E.B. Dubois/ Cornel West

CALL:

Quilombo Enterprises ICM
2311-7th Avenue, Oakland, Ca 94606
(800) 465-7487
Web page: Http://www.cultureshocknews.com
Email: quillombo@earthlink.net

MY BIO-SPHERE

MY BIO-SPHERE

My name is Ian, in England born
My father's from the islands, my mum's from the shore
My youth was spent fleeing xenophobic bores.

I traveled to Athens and Timbuktu
I bathed at Alhambra, Granada, too
I could never shake my brooding school.

My American wife dragged me here,
My stepdaughter in toe, a brand new sphere
My opposition to the States took 10 years to clear.

I started again, from scratch in haste
I started to relearn a new verb, chase
I started to learn a new action, waste.

My endeavors were positive though painfully slow
My dues well paid, eventually did grow
My overnight success took many moons to glow.

I now serve the public, civil and clean
I now work the markets and international scene
I now have great credit and a labyrinth machine.

My writings have covered prose and essays
My heroes are Baldwin, Sojinka and Sessay
My novel attempts include travel and jazzy.

I read like a fish who swims in the night
I spend more on books than I have such a right
I meditate, cool out, and stay un-tight.

My dreams are to learn the heart of the word
My hopes are to chase that winged bird
My endeavors, I pray, are to teach and be heard.

I live in Oakland, city caught in a lie
I dwell in environs of many colored eyes
I inhabit a space of love and deep signs.

My time here now is 18 years plus
My memories of home are short and cussed
My life's irony is to be an English fuss.

Ian C. Moore